MARGRET & H. A. REY'S

Curious George
and the Summer Games

Written by Monica Perez
Illustrated in the style of H. A. Rey by Mary O'Keefe Young

HOUGHTON MIFFLIN HARCOURT
Boston   New York

hmhbooks.com
curiousgeorge.com

The text of this book is set in Garamond.

ISBN: 978-0-358-16410-4 hardcover
ISBN: 978-0-358-24221-5 paperback

Printed in China
SCP 10 9 8 7 6 5 4 3 2 1
4500792103

George was a little monkey who was good at a lot of things . . . especially being curious. What was all that commotion on the field near his home?

The man with the yellow hat told George, "That's the recreation center staff setting up for their summer field day event.

Any kid in town can compete in sports like volleyball or track and field. Each event has a prize—a medal!"

George wanted a medal! He ran onto the field.
His friend quickly followed.

"Come and join us, George! We're practicing for the competition next week." George's neighborhood friends were lined up in front of some strange-looking structures. They looked like huge staples.

A kid named Lorenzo started running and as soon as he reached the first metal bar, he leaped over it. Then he jumped over another and another.

"You want to try the hurdles?" the man asked George. The little monkey nodded eagerly.

The hurdles were too high to leap over. George still had fun, but this was not the sport for him.

George was curious about many
different sports. Next, he tried
the long jump and badminton.

Both sports were harder than
he thought they would be.

Many of the kids had
been participating in
them for months. They
were hard to beat.

"Playing sports is about being fit and healthy, George," the man explained. "And having fun. It's not just about winning." This made George feel better. And since the Summer Games were happening the next weekend, George had the rest of the week to practice.

So he did. Every day.

The next day George joined a volleyball team. He was good at diving for the ball. "Go, George!" his teammates shouted.

But instead of returning the ball over the net with one bump,
George grabbed it and ran . . . Uh-oh.

George would need
to learn so many
rules about this game
before he could play
the right way.

On Wednesday, George returned to the field.

He was curious about the relay race. He saw kids take turns running with a baton around a large oval track. It didn't look too hard . . .

George was assigned the anchor leg,
which meant he would run last.

But he didn't understand he could only take the baton
from his teammate. He took the first baton that came
close—from another team!

The track coach steered the little monkey in the direction
of the gymnastics area.

George tried the balance beam first. He was naturally
good at keeping his balance without wobbling.

He could swing on the rings
without getting tired.

And he was so fast on the
pommel horse he got applause.

He had found his sport!

George spent two more days
practicing his skills with
the other gymnasts on the
West Street Wonder team.

Stella, one of the younger members, showed him how to pirouette on the balance beam. "I bet you're as excited as I am," she said to George. "It's my first competition too."

Finally, the Summer Games arrived.

Gymnastics was up first! George enjoyed cheering on his teammates. Even though he did sometimes forget he shouldn't be doing cartwheels on the sidelines and distracting the audience.

But look—oh no. Stella hadn't started her routine.
She was nervous that there were so many faces
watching from the stands.

George heard someone say Stella had "stage fright."
He knew what he had to do.

Before anyone could tell him it was against the rules, he climbed
onto the beam and did a handstand. Stella smiled at him. George
then held out a hand. Stella stretched her arms out and bowed.
Then she did a perfect pirouette. George mirrored her.

As long as Stella kept her eyes on George, she didn't feel nervous.
She finished her routine to grand applause!

There wasn't a medal for doubles gymnastics, but there were ribbons for team effort. That was just fine with George. Making new friends and learning a sport had been the best part of the Summer Games.

Besides, there was always next year.